Isaac Ray

A Discourse on the Life and Character of Dr. Luther V. Bell

Read to the Association of Superintendents of North American Institutions

for the Insane, at its Annual Meeting, in Providence, R.I., June 10th, 1862

Isaac Ray

A Discourse on the Life and Character of Dr. Luther V. Bell
Read to the Association of Superintendents of North American Institutions for the Insane, at its Annual Meeting, in Providence, R.I., June 10th, 1862

ISBN/EAN: 9783337384043

Printed in Europe, USA, Canada, Australia, Japan

Cover: Foto ©Raphael Reischuk / pixelio.de

More available books at **www.hansebooks.com**

A

DISCOURSE

ON THE

LIFE AND CHARACTER

OF

DR. LUTHER V. BELL,

READ TO THE

ASSOCIATION OF SUPERINTENDENTS

OF NORTH AMERICAN INSTITUTIONS FOR THE INSANE,

AT ITS ANNUAL MEETING, IN PROVIDENCE, R. I.,

June 10th, 1862.

BY

I. RAY, M. D.

BOSTON:
1863.
J. H EASTBURN'S PRESS

At the Annual Meeting of the "Association of Medical Superintendents, of North American Institutions for the Insane," held at Providence, R. I., 10th of June, 1862, the following Resolutions, offered by Dr. Tyler, were adopted.

Resolved: That the members of this Association, have received with emotions of profound sorrow and regret, the announcement of the death of Dr. Luther V. Bell, a past President of this body, and one of the most eminent and distinguished of the many great men, who have adorned the medical profession; that we desire to place upon record, our full and grateful appreciation of his able and unwearied efforts, in diffusing and establishing correct and enlightened views of the nature and treatment of mental disease; that we are deeply impressed with the remembrance of the disinterestedness, kindness, dignity and purity of his character, of his inflexible integrity and singular moral courage, of his extraordinary attainments as a scholar, philosopher, and psychologist, of the wonderful power of his personal influence, of his rare and remarkable attractiveness in social life, and his inestimable worth as a friend and associate; that we recognize with unqualified admiration, in all the acts of his private, professional, and public life, the same unwavering consistency and faithfulness to his convictions of right, in the face of any personal task or sacrifice, which led him, in the exigencies of the day, to give his life to his country, and made him, unconciously to himself, a striking example to us all, of pure, ardent, Christian patriotism.

Resolved: That the Secretary communicate to the family of Dr. Bell, these Resolutions, with the respectful sympathy of the Association.

Immediately after the reading of the resolutions, Dr. Ray was requested, by a vote of the Association, to read a discourse on the Life and Character of Dr. Bell.

DISCOURSE.

I THINK I only entertain the universal sentiment among us, in believing that whatever else we may do or say, on this occasion, we shall welcome the opportunity of turning our thoughts for a while, upon one who held no common place in our respect and affections. We have seen the last of him on earth, whose name was intimately connected with the history of this Association; who, for several years, presided over its deliberations; whose words of wisdom we listened to with the profoundest interest; whose courteous, genial, dignified bearing, drew to him every heart. He has left behind, his services in the cause of philanthropy, of science, and of country, and a character ennobled by the highest order of moral and intellectual endowment. Let us contemplate those services and that character, for the purpose of benefiting ourselves, and of paying to them our grateful tribute of respect and admiration.

DR. BELL was born in New Hampshire, in December, 1806, and consequently was fifty-five years old. His ancestors were among those Irish presbyterians who settled in that State, in the early part of the last century. The family of his own time, has been distinguished by numerous men of mark, honored and trusted in their respective communities, and put into respon-

2

sible places. For many years in fact in that part of the country, his name has been the synonym of ability, integrity, and worth; familiar as household words, on the bench, in the gubernatorial chair, in the Senate of the Union. Before he had finished his seventeenth year, he graduated at Bowdoin College, with a reputation unsullied by any of those follies which students are so apt to mistake for the fruits of spirit and courage. Notwithstanding his youth, he held a respectable rank, in a class of considerably more than the average ability. From college he went to New York, and commenced the study of medicine with his brother, Dr. John Bell, who died a few years after, at the threshold of a most promising career. Having completed his courses and taken his degree, he was induced by his friends, who thought him too young to assume the responsibilities of a physician, to spend a year or little more, in a counting-room, in which, no doubt, he increased his knowledge of men, if not of diseases and remedies. In selecting a field of labor, he was finally led by family reasons, to choose his native place, Chester, but he subsequently changed it for Derry, having married, in the the mean time, Miss Frances Pinkerton.

For five or six years, he was engaged in the trying and arduous duties of a country practitioner. Though long accustomed to the conveniences and amenities of a city life, yet, with that power of accommodation which he possessed in a remarkable degree, he readily submitted to the sacrifices and privations, both social and professional, incident to the country doctor. He shirked no duty, was ready for whatever offered, and left on the minds of the community an abiding impression of his fidelity and skill. Of course, no one the least acquainted with our friend, would suppose that he was merely a routine practitioner, posting through the country, from one patient to another, and dispensing the inevitable drugs, with as little thought as the horse which carried him about. Though never a book-worm, his mind was always active. Nothing escaped his notice, which was worthy of attention, and his observations habitually suggested thought and inquiry. The occurrence of small-pox, in his neighborhood, furnished him some curious facts which served as the basis of a pamphlet entitled, *An attempt to investigate some obscure and undecided doctrines, in relation to small-pox and varioliform diseases.* A year or two before, while Dr. Sylvester Graham was publicly advocating a revolutionary change in the food of mankind, the Trustees of the Boylston Prize Fund propounded as the subject of their annual prize essay, the diet most suitable to the people of New England. For this prize, Dr. Bell successfully tried, in a memoir characterized by original observation and strong practical common sense; and it contributed no doubt, in a great degree, to stay the progress of a delusion which had already produced much mischief.

About this time, the public attention was aroused, on the subject of establishing a hospital for the insane in New Hampshire, and strong efforts were made by the friends of the cause, to induce the Legislature to undertake it. It encountered many obstacles from timid friends and open enemies, and, year after year, was the theme of fruitless talk. To a man like Dr. Bell, always ready to promote any cause of humanity, and to magnify the worth and dignity of his profession, this enterprise was full of interest. For the purpose of giving it more efficient aid than he could in any other way, he offered himself as a candidate for the Legislature, and was elected by a large majority. As chairman of a committee on the projected institution, he made an elaborate report, which, by means of its full statistics, and its appeals to the common humanity and common sense of the community, made a decidedly favorable impression on the public mind. Here his agency in the movement ceased, for just then he was invited to become the superintendent of the McLean asylum, to supply the place of Dr. Lee, lately deceased. It is a striking proof of the high position he had achieved, that this appointment, then second in honor and value to no other of the kind in the country, was entirely unexpected and unsolicited by himself, or his personal friends. With no lack of able and earnest men immediately around them, the Trustees of that institution, comprising a body of shrewd, liberal minded, clear headed men, came to the conclusion that the rising physician in New Hampshire, beyond any other man, possessed the qualifications they sought, and well did the result justify their choice. At the period when he

took charge of the McLean asylum, in 1837, hospitals
for the insane had scarcely passed through the infant
stage. They were few, three only existing in New
England, and the number of their patients so small, as
to show that they were but little appreciated by the
public. The McLean had the prestige of the Massachusetts General Hospital, of which it was an off-shoot;
it had the countenance and support of the elite of a
community second to no other, in point of intelligence
and sagacity, and yet, after eighteen years of trial, it
had less than seventy patients, and was a considerable
charge to the parent institution. When Dr. Bell retired from it, after a service of nearly twenty years, the
number of its patients had nearly trebled, its capacity
was enlarged by new edifices, and it had long been a
self-supporting establishment. His talents and manners
were well calculated to dissipate prejudice, to win the
favor of the thinking classes, and to impress upon all,
the conviction that he was fully adequate to the utmost
requirements of his place. The parent, the child, the
guardian, left in his charge the dearest object of their
affections, well satisfied that they could not have made
a better choice. Liberal men were more readily induced to bestow their bounties, where they were so
sure their application would be judiciously made. A
munificent donation for the purpose of erecting buildings for the accommodation of the more affluent classes,
in a style of appointment never before witnessed in

this country, may be instanced as one of the results of the confidence reposed in his counsels.

During the period of his superintendence, he maintained an active interest in all professional subjects, and especially in such as were directly connected with that to which he was mainly devoted. In hospital architecture he was deeply interested, not only by reason of his mechanical turn, but because he regarded it as intimately connected with the treatment of the insane. And he soon began to feel that here the work of improvement was most needed; that a great reform of the prevalent notions and practices, on this subject, must constitute the first step in any decided advance of our institutions. He saw that in their architectural arrangements, the economical consideration had prevailed, to such a degree, as to essentially compromise the objects for which they were created.

It was not long, before he had an opportunity of offering a practical illustration of his views. In 1844, the Trustees of the Butler hospital, in Providence, R. I. then about to establish an institution for the insane, were desirous, that, as far as practicable, it should embody the improvements of the time, both at home and abroad. In aid of their design, he was readily induced, though in mid-winter, and at considerable personal sacrifice, to sail for Europe, where he visited the principal hospitals of England and France. He was well rewarded for his pains, for he found that in many important respects, they were greatly in advance of ours, and that in their later buildings, many questions of architectural arrangement had been practically answered. He found them taking down hospitals superior to any of ours, and saw, on a large scale, the results of a more liberal expenditure than we had been accustomed to. He was struck with the greater account there made of ample space, light, and dimensions, even in pauper establishments, and was impressed with the salutary influence they must exert on the disordered mind. In regard to internal arrangements, he learned much that was calculated to produce reflection, both as to the sanitary and the economical result. He found, for instance, to his surprise, that associated dormitories, which were hardly known with us, were considered as indispensable to the highest measure of success, and had been introduced into every recently erected establishment. His observations convinced him that in some degree or other, they were worthy of trial by us, though the comparative amount of accommodation of this kind, must vary with the character of the patients. He introduced them into the plan of the Butler hospital, and fifteen years of experience have abundantly confirmed the correctness of his views.

It was in the matter of warming and ventilation, however, that the British institutions exhibited the greatest advance. The furnace, cockle, stove and fireplace, had given way, in many instances, to coils of steam or hot-water pipes, and ventilation was secured by the employment of an artificial force. The immense value of these improvements, he recognized at once, and from that time, he always maintained, that no other method of warming a hospital should be tolerated, and that no kind of ventilation deserved the name, that was not dependent on artificial power. He was also struck by the great account there made, of an agreeable site, and a tasteful style of building, and he ever after placed a high value on those points, for the favorable impression they were calculated to make, both on the sane and the insane.

His report was printed[*], and its suggestions, for the most part, were incorporated into the establishment for whose benefit they were particularly made. That a great and durable advance, was thereby made, in the hospital architecture of our country, no one, I think, will deny. Few, perhaps, would be willing to adopt all his views, and as few would be disposed to reject them all. In fact the old means of warning and ventilation have been generally rejected; the long, dark, narrow corridor, lined on both sides by sleeping-rooms, has given way to one from which the rooms are entirely left out on one side, or partially so, on both; and the associated dormitory has become a prevalent feature of the internal arrangements. A more important service could hardly have been rendered, than this of successfully discrediting the old, hospital model, then invariably used, and supposed to be perfect.

---

* American Jour. Insanity, II., 13.

In the planning of the various hospitals that have since been constructed, in this part of the country, his counsel was generally sought, and though he did not consider himself fully responsible for any of them, yet, his suggestions were always more or less heeded; and sometimes, where he failed to secure the proper arrangement, he did the next best service of preventing some wretched conceptions of an ambitious builder or building-committee, from being embodied in brick and mortar. I need scarcely remind you how seldom it happens, that the plans of an expert are executed completely and in good faith, and therefore, before visiting the defects of a building on him whose name is connected with its plans, it is but fair to inquire how far they were modified by others.

In 1848, he was elected to deliver the anniversary discourse before the Massachusetts Medical Society. He chose the subject which then much occupied his thoughts, and which he regarded as vastly important in its hygienic relations:—that of warming and ventilation. It was an admirable résumé of the modern progress in those arts, and made more valuable by original suggestions. When published, it was enlarged by the addition of many details, and will long continue to be consulted by the practical student.

In 1857, he was elected President of the above-named Society, the roll of his predecessors embracing many a name, associated with high conceptions of learning, skill, and worth.

His professional eminence, in a community not slow to recognize the fact in all its important bearings, led to his employment, to an unexpected degree, in judicial investigations involving questions of mental condition. This kind of cases, as we are all aware, has been getting more and more common; and thus, to one whose reputation renders his opinion peculiarly valuable, this forensic service makes no trifling addition of care and responsibility. During the last dozen years of his life, no inconsiderable part of his time was spent in the court-room — much of it in the service of the poor and helpless. Nowhere scarcely will he be more missed than in the Courts of Massachusetts, where his frequent presence had not the effect of cheapening his opinion in the estimate of the legal profession.

In 1853, he was appointed one of a Board of Commissioners for examining convicts in the Penitentiary who presented indications of mental disease. No professional duty could draw more largely on his abundant resources than this. It required, for an important practical purpose, the application of all his tact and discernment — all his knowledge of disease and all his knowledge of men, with a result that was sure to be tested by time. To be baffled occasionally by the devices of some arch deceiver whose whole life may have been devoted to the practice of all manner of deceit and iniquity, would imply no culpable defect of skill, but I am not aware that in a single instance during his long service on this commission, his conclusion was falsified by the final event.

In 1850, he was chosen a member of the Executive Council of the State. Among the duties of this body is that of advising the Governor in cases of application for the pardon of criminals under sentence. While serving in this capacity, he was selected by his associates to examine and report upon the case of Dr. Webster, then under sentence of death for the murder of Dr. Parkman. After trying every other means which the laws allowed, his friends appealed to this tribunal of the last resort, in the hope of obtaining from men who would be governed, in some degree, by the common views and feelings of humanity, what was refused by those who were actuated by no other consideration than the rules of evidence and the settled principles of law. To show that there was nothing in the facts they presented to warrant the Governor in disturbing the verdict already pronounced by the jury and by public opinion, was a duty most painful to one of his feelings and position; but, nevertheless, it was most ably and conscientiously discharged. Whatever doubt may have existed as to the correctness of this decision, it was thoroughly removed by subsequent revelations. At the same time there was assigned to him the examination of another application for pardon. in which he displayed that happy combination of professional sagacity, clear perceptions, and rectitude of purpose, which formed such prominent traits in his character. The prisoner, subsequent to the act, had shown signs of dementia, which, taken in connection with some obscurity in the circumstances of the murder, led to a strong suspicion, if not belief, that the man was insane. The evidence to this effect was strong enough to confirm the natural repugnance to capital punishment; but Dr. Bell who had heard the evidence given on the trial, was quite satisfied that all the pretended signs of insanity were simulated, and this view of the case was enforced with his usual clearness, in his report. The correctness of this opinion was subsequently confirmed by the confession of the man that he had been simulating mental disease.

The interest manifested by Dr. Bell in Spiritualism, as it is called, is known to us all; for twice he made it the subject of a paper which was read to this Association. Availing himself of some peculiarly favorable opportunities for witnessing the Spiritual performances, he commenced a series of systematic investigations into this pretended new power. To this duty he was prompted both by his psychological studies, and his peculiar turn of mind. He believed it to be within the limits of legitimate scientific inquiry, and well worthy the attention of those whose special province it is to study the mind, both in the normal and the abnormal state. It is not strange that one who, for so many years, had been devoted to this study, should have been strongly moved by the accounts which daily came to his ears, of performances among his neighbors, some of whom were his most respected and intelligent friends, that indicated apparently some psychological agency which, if not new and original, was strange and curious. Indeed, he felt that he would be false to his professional trust if he neglected to improve the opportunity thus placed before him, for the good of science and humanity. Whether it occurred to him, at the start, that the performance of this duty might subject him to the ridicule and reproach of men whose good opinion he highly prized, I cannot say; but I am quite sure that such anticipations would not have deterred him for a single moment. In this spirit he attended the sittings, took an active part in the proceedings, subjected the manifestations to various tests, and made himself thoroughly acquainted with the new art. The time, the patience, the effort, necessary for this purpose, implied a degree of scientific zeal worthy of admiration, even if it had been devoid of valuable results. He was satisfied, however, that he had discovered some of the laws by which these manifestations are controlled; and though very far from regarding them as the exclusive offspring of humbug and fraud, he saw no proof of supernatural, preternatural, or spiritual agency. In a letter written shortly before his death, he emphatically declares: "I never was a believer in Spiritualism; on the contrary, I always supposed I did as much as any man in New England to put a stop to that gigantic epidemic, by demonstrating that its facts were only those of old Mesmerism, &c., and that the mediums never told what the inquirer did not know before." This ought to be sufficient, if nothing else, to remove a prevalent misapprehension concerning his views on this subject, created, partly, no doubt, by the position he was sometimes obliged to assume towards the adversaries of Spiritualism. He thought some of them pursued their investigations rather in the spirit of hostile partizans than of sincere, philosophical seekers after truth ; and such a course was repugnant to all his ideas of fair dealing and of a truly scientific inquiry. Considering that the subject was regarded by scientific men with a feeling of contempt which deterred them from serious or faithful inquiry, and by speculative or undisciplined minds with a kind of credulity that invited imposition, it must ever be considered as fortunate that a shrewd and cautious observer, trained to the strictest rules of scientific research, should have entered upon its investigation with the requisite patience and zeal, and a hearty willingness to receive the truth, whatever it might be. He published nothing himself, but the papers read here, and some communications to writers of books would make a valuable contribution to our knowledge.

For several years before he left the McLean asylum, he devoted considerable attention to politics. Belonging to a family which, had always taken a prominent part in public affairs, he naturally looked with favor and some longing, on a field of action in which so many of those nearest him in blood and affection, had distinguished themselves, and done the State some service. He attended conventions, prepared resolutions and addresses, and occasionally spoke. He was a member of the Baltimore Convention which nominated General Scott for the Presidency, and in the course of a speech in Faneuil Hall, respecting the doings of the Convention, he forgot, for a moment, the party-politician, and launched into a hearty tribute to the honesty of his old friend and companion, General Pierce, the opposing candidate. Such a deviation from the ordinary tactics showed pretty clearly that he was lacking an important element of political success. In 1852, he was a candidate for Congress, and in 1856, for the office of Governor. The party by which he was nominated,—the old Whig party, to whose fortunes he faithfully clung amid the most sweeping desertions,—was too small to give him more than a lean minority of votes.

For five years he was the President of this Association, and was always deeply interested in its success. He spared no pains to promote its usefulness, because he regarded it as a most efficient instrumentality for elevating the condition of our establishments for the insane. He took a foremost part in our discussions, and I need only remind you of the delight with which we listened, year after year, to the glowing words which bore witness of the warm philanthropist, the sagacious physician, and the profound psychologist. I

may safely say that he never spoke without saying
something we would not willingly forget; and among
the pleasing reminiscences connected with our meetings, treasured up in the mind of every member, will
be, I doubt not, some memorable utterance of our
departed associate.

In 1856, after a service of nearly twenty years, he
retired from the McLean asylum, and thenceforth
resided in the neighboring town of Charlestown, under
the shadow of Bunker Hill, where the first object that
greeted his opening eyes in the morning light, was the
scene of his best labors, of his highest enjoyments, and
of his deepest sorrows. Within the few previous
years, his home had been made desolate by the death
of his wife and three children, one of them, his eldest
son, then in college; and now the care of his four
remaining children became the favorite object of his
life. The state of his health, which had been weakened by repeated attacks of pneumonia and hemopty-
sis, from which, more than once, his recovery was
regarded as impossible, seemed to forbid any arduous
exertions. Much of his time was given to consulta-
tions with other physicians, to attendance on trials, as
an expert, and much of it to politics. A new scene,
however, was soon to open, in which this feeble invalid, whom the winds of heaven were not allowed to
visit too roughly, was destined, under the spur of a
noble sentiment, to encounter exposure, privation and
toil, unknown to his most vigorous years. In that

great crisis of our affairs which was to try men's souls
as they were never tried before, he needed no second
thought to determine what part he should take. By
nature and by education, by principle and by feeling,
a friend to law and order, and a lover of his country,
he sprung at once to the support of the Government,
without caring to see who stood beside him. He
talked with his neighbors, he spoke in public meetings,
he wrote in the newspapers. What more could be
expected of one who, for several years, had been regarded as holding upon life by the feeblest of tenures—
of one who had suffered repeated attacks of pulmonary
hemorrhage, who had been brought to death's door by
pleurisy and pneumonia, and one of whose lungs was
quite impervious to air? It was not enough for him.
He felt that in the impending conflict no man should be
idle. No pressure of duty kept him at home ; he was
conscious of possessing talents and skill that would be
of service to the cause; and his example would have its
weight at a time when men, just recovering from their
surprise and stupor, were earnestly watching the move-
ments of one another. Abandoning the little circle that
had become inexpressibly dear to his affections, and renouncing all the little appliances of comfort which had
seemed indispensable to his invalid condition, he offered
his services to the Governor of the State, on the 10th
of June, received his commission as Surgeon of the
11th Regiment of Massachusetts Volunteers, and left
with it for Washington on the 30th of June. His

regiment was soon removed to the Virginia side of the river, and took its full share in the disastrous battle of Bull Run. He established himself in Sudley church, and from 2 to 7, P. M., he was engaged in performing operations. On the retreat of the army, it became a question with him and his assistants whether they should join it, or remain and be captured with their patients. At first he decided to stay, and kept at work until it became apparent to everybody else that they would only be adding themselves to the sacrifice of their wounded men. After encountering many perils and hair-breadth escapes, he reached Washington the next day, with a disorganized, panic-stricken host of fugitives.*

* Dr. Bell's account of his escape, contained in a letter to a friend, is worth preserving, in a notice of this kind : "About 7, P, M., C. got my attention, and said that if I expected to change my decision, now was the time, for the enemy was upon us. I thought about half a day's work in one minute. On one side rose up the idea of abandoning the wounded, six or eight cases of whom I had laid aside, to be next amputated ; of the possible blame of a surgeon's leaving his post of duty in a presumptively civilized country. On the other side was the unanimous cry from all around that we should not be spared, for our red hospital-flag was utterly lost in the mass of red zouave blankets piled everywhere round the outside steps of the church. It was almost certain, too, that even our own troops rushing red-handed for a victorious pursuit, would not have stayed to think of surgeons or wounded, and why then should the more ignorant, Southern, low whites spare us ? C. said we had been here alone for an hour. Dr. M., of the Regular Army, fled long before, saying to C. that he was a Virginian, and would suffer doubly if caught ; and the New York Zouave doctor, after ostentatiously cutting off a thigh near the body, (a perfectly useless operation,) cleared. I then said that it was our duty to go, unscrewed a tourniquet, threw down the knife, put on my soldier's coat and scarf, and went off through a creek and up a hill, and joined the mighty throng bearing away with the utmost speed and panic, probably 20,000 in number, with artillery, cavalry and baggage-wagons, all crowded to-

His regiment was now ordered to Maryland, and made a part of General Hooker's Division. Shortly after, he was appointed Brigade Surgeon, and finally, Division Surgeon. Up to the last week of his life, his health and power of endurance steadily improved under the hardships and privations of the camp. And yet he took them as they came, making no attempt to favor himself by unusual privileges. During his whole period of service in Maryland, he slept out of camp but one night. "Seven nights," he says, in a letter to the writer, "I slept beneath the canopy of heaven [in Virginia;] twice I was on horseback, or on foot, behind my marching regiment, over twenty-four hours in succession. For a week I was happy to dip up

gether. Once in a while a report came that the foe was upon us. I believe some cavalry did pursue. At one accord, every body rushed at right and left through the wood; then soon became re-assured, and got into the wide road through the forest, for it was woods every mile of the way, from Bull Run to Fairfax Court-house. I lost the excellent horse which P. bought — a horse of every suitable quality for my use — my sword, belt, Sammy's shawl, and brother James's revolver. When I left the church, I was almost exhausted with operating and dressing for five hours. We got out of everything — water, stimulants, dressings. Of course, with my short wind, I was in a bad state for a race. I begged them to leave me and look out for themselves; but with one accord they refused. Still we were all separated, within ten minutes after, by one of the panic reports which compelled every man to float along the rushing current in which he formed an atom. After working along two or three miles in this way, I was recognized by a man to whom I shall always be under infinite obligations. He was our mess-cook, W. A. B., a New Hampshire man. [He had received some attentions from Dr. B., on account of a surgical disease.] This and a few words of civil kindness were all the claim I had on him, yet if he had been my own son, he could not have done more, or made more sacrifices for me. He insisted on getting off a horse he had got, and putting me on him. Afterwards, we took up a sick officer, Lieut. S., and we rode double, as was the general fashion that night. When we had water to drink from a warm and muddy brook, in a dirty tin dipper, between my horse's fore feet and mouth. I have had but one sick day, and have been cheerful and happy." It was consonant to all his notions of professional duty, to believe that all his time and all his powers belonged to the service he had undertaken. The idea of making his office subservient to any other object than the welfare of the troops, was as far from his thoughts as the poles are asunder. In a letter to a friend, he says: "In conformity to a principle laid down from the beginning, for my conduct, I have never waited for a second call, night or day, real or sham, bona fide or imaginary."

scampered on some five or six miles, we reached a narrow, high Virginia bridge, over Cub Run, with a deep water-way at its side, On it and in the water, was an absolute jam of cannons, wagons, ambulances, cavalry, soldiers, &c., all crushed together in a fixed mass. At the instant, one of the enemy's rifled cannon — no doubt the range was fixed by daylight — began to pour in shells, with the most awful, whizzing, bursting sound you can conceive of. Gus, as my savior-friend was called for shortness, (his middle name being Augustus,) seized our horse by the bridle, and crowded him off into the side-woods. After going parallel to the woods a few rods, he left us to search for a passage by the bridge, while S. and I crossed an open clearing, hoping to cross the creek below the bridge. As we neared it, a cordon of trees and steep banks showed that it could only be crossed elsewhere, or on foot. We decided to abandon the horse just as another shell crashed down the trees near us. S. slipped off just at that moment, but Gus cried to me to stick by the horse and come to the bridge. I did so, and surmounted a stone wall, four feet high, to reach the water-way. Gus tumbled an ambulance out of the way, and, with a sword he had picked up, urged on the horse, who insisted on halting to drink. One of our regiment belabored him behind with a bayonet, and at last he mounted the steep bank and got out. After proceeding to the top of the hill, S., who had crossed the creek below, by a strange coincidence, rejoined us, and remounted. When we reached Fairfax Court-house, (Gus walking all the way,) he hired for me a seat in a lager-beer wagon, to Columbia Springs, opposite Washington, and I lost him on the road."

The transformation wrought in his habits, his feelings, and his powers, by his military experience, was no less surprising to himself than to others. In December, 1861, he writes: "The date of this letter brings strongly to my mind the fact that I am going on rapidly to the close of the first half year of my soldiering life. I think it was about the 10th of June that I was appointed and began to make ready. How eventful! how strange! how dreamlike! does this last half-year of life seem to me. Sometimes when I go 'a reviewing' with the General, and we all start off at a furious trot, down one side of the brigade and up behind, dressed up with gold livery, long boots and spurs, and all the 'other little et ceteras' of the pomp and circumstance of war, the feeling crosses me that I am not 'in the form,' as the spiritualists term it, but have entered on some new plane or sphere of existence. I find myself, too, growing anxious for a fight. I ride down to the river to watch the exchange of shots, without the slightest thought that I may be the predestinated victim of one of those awfully murderous missiles of which our troops have already picked up enough to stock a museum. Still, the months have passed away rapidly, and almost without an obstacle. I have been uniformly treated, personally, from the Major-General down to the drummer-boy, with all the respect I could desire."

Some idea of the discomforts he endured, of a kind not supposed to be very conducive to the health of an invalid, may be gathered from a letter dated at Bladensburgh, August 13th. "We have now been at this spot, infamous as the site of the infamous race of 1814, and of all the principal duels for the last half century, ten days, and are pretty well settled down; for it takes a week or so after a move, to get the tents gathered, booths over the camp-kettles, &c. I have had my tent floored over with rough boards, and have kept dry as far as outside water is concerned, although it has rained almost daily; still, everything is perfectly saturated with water, so that it is not very easy to write legibly on this good sheet of paper, with a good pen, and good ink; in fact, it is living out of doors to all intents and purposes. But I am uniformly well. I am fully trying—what I had in view, from the first—Dr. Marshall Hall's theory of treating pulmonary disease, by living in a hut through every crack of which the stars can be seen." He began, at last, to think that his experiment had proved a hygienic success, and the future was full of hope and satisfaction, when suddenly the scene changed. On the morning of February the 5th, having gone to bed in his usual condition, he was awakened by intense pains in his chest, which, at first, seemed to be rheumatic. In the course of a day or two, dyspnœa came on, when his medical attendant, Dr. Foye, diagnosed pericarditis. In the midst of the severest pains he continued calm and self-possessed, saw clearly the inevitable result, said he had no messages to send, no orders to give, for he had provided for everything:

and thus, quietly, without ostentation, a life, devoted to the cause of humanity and science, was beautifully finished by a death in the service of his country. Fortunate life! Fortunate death! Seldom are the various parts and phases of a career so admirably fitted and proportioned one to another, leaving nothing to be desired, nothing to be regretted.

Such were the principal events in the life of our friend and associate. Such were the various relations which he sustained towards his fellow men; and it becomes us now to consider how he sustained them.

The principal of these, that in which he performed the greatest service and achieved the most of his reputation, was, unquestionably, his superintendence of a hospital for the insane. In assuming this office, he aimed for the best and highest results which it was capable of affording. Never had any man higher notions of the worth and dignity of his calling, of its power of exercising the noblest faculties, of its fitness for elevating and strengthening the character. He was not one of those who are contented with that respectable measure of success which ensures their continuance in office. He felt that the field of effort on which he had entered was ready, not only to yield the obvious and ordinary fruits that might be expected, but to reward the loftiest ambition and the most earnest purpose. To his view it was as broad as the immense range of medical and mental science can make it, and as inexhaustible as the wants of suffering humanity.

28

When he entered upon it, hospitals for the insane were little more than an experiment upon the intelligence of the people. To remove a sufferer of the saddest description, from the ministrations of friends to the mercenary care of strangers, at the very moment, of all others, when he seems most to need that protection which the ties of nature alone can furnish, is a step not so easily taken then as now. The advantages of such institutions might be abstractly admitted, even, by many a one who, practically, yielded to prejudice and suspicion. The consequence was that for the most part, patients were consigned to them with fear and trembling; that the number of patients was small, and the institutions themselves languishing for lack of the proper support. And so imperfectly did those who were intrusted with their general supervision understand the working of the instrumentality placed in their hands, that the efficiency of means merely moral was scarcely recognized. Food, lodging, and custody were regarded as the principal things; and, in fact, there was little else beside. Scarcely a single article of furniture was allowed beyond the strong, heavy fixtures absolutely required by the service. Almost every object that met the eye had a peculiar if not a forbidding aspect. True, a step in the right direction had been taken at the start, by the Trustees of the McLean asylum, in selecting for their establishment the country-seat of an affluent gentleman, having a beautiful garden in front and an agreeable prospect on every side. But the idea thus recognized was not rapidly developed, partly, no doubt, for the want of means, and partly for the want of a proper appreciation of its importance. The object proposed by these institutions was the relief of disordered minds; and yet it is wonderful how few of their appliances were addressed directly to the mind. Not a great many years ago, one might have visited every hospital from Maine to Georgia, without finding a picture, a billiard table, a bowling alley, or a library, within their premises. This defect Dr. Bell observed and deplored, and his opinion of medication tended to make him think more earnestly respecting it. He had little faith in the efficacy of drugs in the treatment of insanity, and during the latter part of his life, seldom gave them except to meet those ailments that generally accompany it. He had no theory on the subject. His views were the result of observation, for at first he resorted freely to the medication then in vogue. The hackneyed argument, that insanity being a disease of a bodily organ, is therefore as proper a subject of medication as any other disease, did not convince him. He saw a fundamental fallacy in the idea that the cure of any disease necessarily implies the use of drugs. He believed, thoroughly and practically, what many physicians believe only speculatively, that the animal economy is endowed with recuperative powers sufficient, in the large majority of cases, to restore it sound and whole from the attacks of disease. Accordingly. he thought the physician should be cautious how he interfered with the restorative processes of nature, and should reserve such interference, until he had substantial reasons for believing that his aid was required. It was enough for him, however, that the results of experience did not warrant much reliance on medical treatment. He did not see that the prescription of any drug or combination of drugs, was often followed, shortly after, by recovery; and he believed that the benefits of a merely tentative medication were more than counterbalanced, in the long run, by some positive mischief. And who of us, in fact, at times, if not habitually, has not found himself driven to the conclusion, with a feeling of mortification and dismay, that after all our efforts, after all our advances, our medication in the treatment of insanity — that, I mean, which is directed immediately to the cerebral affection — is no more successful, than that of our fathers before us? If we have improved at all upon them, does not the improvement consist, rather in discarding their favorite remedies, than in substituting better ones of our own? We see the folly of their emetics, their purges, their mercury, their bleedings, their blisters; but are we ready, with any degree of self-gratulation, to point to opium, or antimony, or hashish, or warm-baths, as *our* means of triumphant success? Dr. Bell was not opposed to the use of drugs because they were drugs, but because he was not satisfied with the evidence of their efficacy. Until, therefore.

the progress of discovery should put us in possession
of surer remedies than any now known to us, he was
disposed, very properly, to rely on what he regarded
as more efficient means. He believed, and he always
believed, that in the management of all diseases,
moral appliances — those which are addressed to some
faculty of the mind — possessed a potency not dis-
tinctly recognized in the prevalent therapeutics of our
time or any time. Indeed, every reflecting and candid
physician must admit, that in his repertory of remarkable and unexpected recoveries, those which can fairly
be attributed to the prescription of drugs, are greatly
outnumbered by such as followed some measure affecting, more or less directly, the moral faculties. To treat
insanity with moral means, chiefly, implies no abne-
gation of its physical origin, for the simple reason, were
there no other, that they are found more or less efficient, in the treatment of diseases unquestionably
physical. Himself a frequent subject of disease, he
recognized in his own personal experience the truth
of this fact, long before it was so remarkably illustrated
in the last year of his life. He did not refuse drugs
altogether. On the contrary, he was rather willing to
take them, but always declared that their efficacy,
when they had any, arose less from any direct action
upon the suffering organs, than from the confidence
and hope which they inspired. I wish to feel, he would
say, that the remedies I am taking, are of no doubtful
value — things that may be dispensed with altogether,

without materially affecting the result — but are precisely what I need to make me well, and to be taken with the strictest regard to the directions of the physician. Holding these views, it followed of course, that he should insist on the paramount importance of moral as compared with medical treatment, and that his efforts should have been directed to its development, in the institution under his charge. Whatever was calculated to produce a pleasing impression on the mind, to turn the thoughts from that morbid introspection, in which the insane so much indulge, to maintain the normal tastes and aptitudes, to excite a healthy interest in the outward world, and bring into play emotions and thoughts that had been stifled by disease, he regarded as worthy of a place in a hospital for the insane. With the aid of generous benefactors, ready to heed his suggestions, he had the satisfaction of knowing, when he quitted the scene of his principal labors, that it was furnished with appliances of this nature, to a degree altogether unequalled in this part of the country.

In his intercourse with his patients, the great variety of his knowledge, both of men and things, always furnished him with some topic of conversation which engaged their attention and rendered his visits agreeable. With no arts of address to strike the fancy, yet his easy and courteous demeanor, and his frank, good-natured manner, secured, in no ordinary degree, their esteem and confidence. With the most perfect control of his feelings, even under the severest provocations, he always maintained that happy blending of firmness and gentleness which is essential to the superintendent of the insane. With inexhaustible patience he listened to their long stories, and manifested an unaffected interest in their troubles. If he could not grant their requests, nor acquiesce in their conclusions, his unfailing tact deprived the unwelcome words of half their rigor. While convalescent, they looked up to him as to a safe counsellor and friend, and among his warmest friends were many who had recovered under his care. In the still more difficult task of obtaining the confidence and co-operation of the friends, he had a measure of success, which, I presume, has seldom if ever, been surpassed. This result was attributable chiefly to his habitual urbanity, and a certain command of intellect that was quite irresistible, even by those who could least comprehend the nature of the influence by which they were controlled. People of all sorts and conditions went away from an interview, with the conviction that their afflicted friends were in the hands of a kind, wise, and considerate man. This is a merit that can be fully appreciated only by considering the great variety of persons with whom he was brought into contact, embracing almost every gradation of manners, morals, and understanding; and no one here needs to be told, that the prejudices and short-sightedness of the ignorant are not more difficult to manage, than the restlessness and distrust of the cultivated classes, which spring from a more exacting spirit, and a more self-

reliant judgment. Fortunate is the man who, in such
a position, can satisfy such a variety of tempers, without compromising his integrity or his self-respect.

In his annual reports, he took the opportunity, not
only to expose the operations of the asylum, but to
enlighten the public on questions of practical importance, connected with mental disease. Scarcely any
one was entirely overlooked, in the course of the nineteen reports made during his term of office; and the
wisdom of his views, springing, as they did, from an
ample personal experience, strong practical common
sense, and a vigorous intellect, will secure for them a
permanent place, in the literature of insanity. The little account made of statistics, by which they were always
characterized, was the result of no hasty, nor superficial
investigation. Carefully and deliberately he arrived
at the belief, that the statements of our specialty had
not that precision and accuracy, necessary to a statistical shape, and that the attempt to give them such a
shape would be a prolific source of uncertainty and
error. Not that many of these facts might not be
profitably reduced to a numerical expression, especially
after a considerable scope and period of observation.
The precise objection, is that many other facts, or
quasi facts, are of doubtful accuracy or of questionable
importance, and that the results of a single year, however correct, can have no statistical value. Under a
great show of knowledge, we get but little that can be
relied on, as the basis of any general principles, and

that little, it was not always easy to distinguish from the much that is merely a matter of personal opinion, rather than precise and tangible fact. His reports also indicated, what was abundantly manifested in his conversations and his other writings, that he was no servile follower of other men, but was able and willing to observe for himself, and had the courage to publish his conclusions, whether likely to be received or rejected. The marks of this originality and independence are visible on every page, and impart a peculiar interest to his writings.

Of his capacity for original observation and scientific discrimination, we had an inestimable proof in the paper which he read to us, in 1849, "*On a form of disease resembling some advanced stages of mania and fever, but so contra-distinguished from any ordinarily observed or described combination of symptoms, as to render it probable, that it may be an overlooked and hitherto unrecorded malady.*" The conclusions to which he there arrived may not be fully confirmed, but the general proposition, that insanity, as popularly understood, embraces some forms of cerebral disease that ought to be distinguished from it, both pathologically and therapeutically, is now, I believe, universally accepted. The necessity and importance of this distinction cannot be disputed, and Dr. Bell is entitled to all the credit that belongs to the first and principal attempt to establish it.

Any account of the professional character of Dr. Bell, would be grossly imperfect, which should overlook his performance in a field of duty, to which he was often summoned,—that of medical expert, in courts of justice. No man, living or dead, ever performed so large an amount of this duty, and I am sure I speak the common sentiment of doctors and lawyers, in saying, that no man ever did it better. A better model for imitation one could hardly propose to himself, for he displayed, in the highest degree, those traits that should always characterize the medical witness. Nothing short of this could have sustained his reputation, and preserved the public confidence, under his frequent appearance in this capacity. Pretension, self-conceit, superficial attainments, may succeed occasionally, but are sure to be recognized and despised, if sufficient opportunity is afforded. The court and the bar, making every deduction which the circumstances of the case require, soon arrived at correct conclusions on this point. And thus it was, that year after year, for a quarter of a century, his opinion was sought; and it often determined the question of life or death, wealth or poverty.

It may be instructive to us all, to consider the grounds of this remarkable success. Undoubtedly, the principal one was the fulness and accuracy of his knowledge, and the promptitude with which he could command it. It was scarcely possible to suppose a question for which he was not ready, his rich experience and strong sagacity amply supplying him with suggestions and points of comparisons germane to the matter in hand. He seized the prominent features of the case, distinguished between the clear and the obscure, and having made up his mind, was ready to testify according to his convictions, without hesitation or embarrassment. Many an expert fails, simply because he is not fully satisfied in his own mind, or is not perfectly sure of the ground before him; counsel see that he is proceeding with uncertain steps, and but little ingenuity is required to disconcert him altogether. In this particular, Dr. Bell never failed. He was always very careful to make up his mind as to what, in the case, was a matter of certainty, and what was a matter of doubt, and then he was able to testify without hesitation or misgiving. He took care also not to be drawn into careless admissions, in order to avoid a fancied dilemma, or to fortify a previous statement.

Our mode of legal procedure provides the worst possible way for obtaining the opinions of experts, because what ought to be a deliberate, dispassionate, well-matured judgment, for the benefit of all concerned, is really an extemporaneous, and perhaps, unpremeditated utterance, intended for the benefit of one side alone. This defect I know it was his endeavor, in practice, to remedy as far as possible, by keeping his mind free from partizan influences; and, though supposed to be in the interest of one side only, regarding himself as a minister of science rather than the servant of a party. Accordingly, if he entertained any

6

doubt, he frankly said so; if he felt himself utterly ignorant on some speculative point started for the purpose of embarrassing him, he made no attempt to conceal it. What he knew and firmly believed, that he declared, whichever side it might affect. Frequently, his testimony was given very much in the style of a report or a scientific discussion, with an air of earnestness and sincerity that won the assent of court and jury. Thus he avoided giving the impression, not unfrequently made by medical testimony, that the expert is struggling under difficulties he cannot remove and will not acknowledge. His facility of expression enabled him always to say precisely what he meant, and his unceasing presence of mind preserved him from embarrassments which, men less fortunately constituted or disciplined, are liable to fall into.

It was also one of the causes of his success, that he properly appreciated the true function of the medical expert. Fully recognizing the fact that what the court and jury want is sound and accurate information within the legal rules of evidence, and knowing that a modest and cautious demeanor is more indicative of these qualities than an air of dogmatism, he never was led into that besetting sin of inexperienced or short-sighted witnesses — making a display of himself. Better perhaps than any other man of our time, he hit the happy medium between saying too much and saying too little — between the meagre utterances

which indicate the suspicion of a trap in every question, and the amplifications of a popular lecture. His
clear conceptions led him to a clearness of statement
which greatly contributed to recommend his opinions;
for people are ever more ready to believe a speaker
who shows that he thoroughly understands himself,
than one whose obscurity of expression seems to reflect
the obscurity of his thoughts. The arts of ingenious
counsel to embarrass him by raising false issues, or
forcing him into false positions, seldom succeeded,
for his quickness of apprehension enabled him to
see the snare in season to avoid it. He had too much
self-respect, too high a sense of his office as an expert,
to bandy words, or try conclusions, with counsel, never
forgetting that his business was, not to contend in a
strife of words, but to declare, simply and briefly, for
the benefit of court and jury, what he believed to be
the truth respecting the case in hand. In fact, counsel
did not often venture upon attempts of the kind just
mentioned, for it was found that they were more likely
to result in disconcerting themselves than the witness.
As little effect was produced upon him by those coarser
attempts to embarrass the expert, in which counsel,
who are ever ready to sink the gentleman in the advo-
cate, occasionally indulge, though a harder trial of
patience to a man of spirit it is difficult to conceive.

It would greatly exceed the limits of this discourse,
to consider the character of Dr. Bell in all the relations which he sustained to society; but there was one

in which the higher qualities of the man were so beautifully displayed, that it would do much injustice both to him and to us, to overlook it altogether. As I have already stated, he manifested much interest in public affairs, and of late was desirous of serving his fellow-citizens in some public capacity. He mingled with politicians, he was made acquainted with the hidden springs of party-movements, he saw the heartlessness and selfishness which pervade the political world; yet it repressed in him no generous emotion, it never chilled the warmth of his friendship, it never weakened his faith in the supremacy of the right, it never turned him a hair's breadth from the line of his integrity. He sought office, not for emolument or distinction, but for the opportunity it afforded of using his powers in some newer field of effort, of studying mankind under new relations, of developing better plans and higher principles in the performance of his allotted work. Had he been successful in obtaining office, and enjoyed a tolerable share of health, we should, undoubtedly, have witnessed the same vigor of thought, the same independence of outside influences, the same constant striving for improvement, which characterized him in all his other relations. At last. just before his sun went down, Providence vouchsafed to him an opportunity of displaying, in some adequate degree, those noble qualities of character which had not been so prominently called for in any previous sphere of duty. Though acting with a party that opposed the election of the men now in power, and not free, I presume, from those feelings of estrangement which opposing parties always entertain towards each other, he declared his readiness to act with any set of men who regarded the preservation of the Union as paramount to every other object. Cold, philosophical, and utterly destitute of sentiment, as he seemed to many who thought they knew him well, yet the warmth of his expressions reminds us of that lofty patriotism which the poet and historian have always loved to describe, for the honor and glory of our race. Within a month of his death, he said, in a letter to a friend: " I never had the beginning of a regret at my decision to devote what may be left of life and ability to the great cause. I have, as you know, four motherless children. Painful as it is to leave such a charge, even in the worthiest hands, I have been forced to it by the reflection, that the great issue, under the stern arbitrament of arms, is, whether or not our children are to have a country."

Strong as his preferences had been for the men and the measures of his party, to which he faithfully clung long after it had almost ceased to have a recognized existence, still more strongly was he moved by any attempt to revive old issues while the very life of the nation was at stake. At the time when the various political parties of his State were nominating candidates for the next election, he expressed his sentiments on the subject. without any mingling of

rose-water. "I can conceive of nothing," he writes to
a friend, "more ineffably stupid, than that any set
of politicians, Democratic or Bell-Everett, should go
through the farce of nominating, or indeed of making
any opposition. The one great cause of nationality or
despotism, of life or death, of having property or
being stripped of everything, so palpably throws all
and every former question of political difference into
entire nothingness, that one can only think of men
who meet in Convention, and pass such resolutions as
the Worcester lot, or even those at our Charlestown
caucus, in the words applied to the old Bourbons,—
'They learned nothing and forgot nothing.' Were I
at home I would go resolutely for the present Executive, as the highest duty, and for the support of those
means and men that went most fully for a vigorous
prosecution of this war, until, if necessary, South Caro-
lina and a dozen more like her, should be blotted from
the map of the Union, as States, and, with the private
estates within their borders, re-divided by the sur-
veyor's chain and compass, and distributed to new
settlers.   *   *   *   I have seen nothing which has
occasioned me so much disquiet as the folly of a few
Democratic 'dead and alive,' of former years. I was
glad to see, by noticing your name as a delegate to
the Union Republican Convention, that our party had
not fallen into such ridiculous fatuity." The idea of
men living at ease and scarcely feeling the pressure of
the tremendous conflict, endeavoring, by some paltry

political device, to divert the public attention from it
to themselves, while he was renouncing all those objects which men hold most dear, seemed to him deserv-
ing of the deepest contempt and indignation.

It may be justly inferred from what has been said,
that Dr. Bell's intellectual powers were of a superior
order, and would have made him eminent in any
calling he might have selected. His choice of a profession was probably determined by what seemed to
be the leading quality of his mind — that kind of
practical sagacity which delights in tangible results
rather than speculative conclusions. In physical science only could his mind find appropriate materials for
its activity, since all its processes are eminently induc-
tive. He had no taste for refined speculation, and of
course often failed to appreciate it properly. Its frequent barrenness of any visible fruit impressed him
more deeply than its pregnant suggestions; and his
habitual belief was that it had no proper place in the
pursuit of physical science. The march of his own
mind was marked by no erratic deviations, but always
led straight on to its object by sure and steady steps.
Under his clear and penetrating insight, things appeared as they really were, stripped of all the devices and disguises in which fancy or sophistry or
falsehood had arrayed them. Plausible theories, high-
sounding pretensions, showy parade, never imposed
upon him, nor was he disposed to receive anything
on the mere strength of prescription or authority.

Novelty had no intrinsic charms for him, and he was habitually inclined to adhere to what he already possessed, until quite sure that a better was offered in its place. When satisfied, however, that a thing was true and worthy of all acceptation, he was not the man to be deterred from receiving and supporting it, by the opposition of the simple or the wise. In fact, a prominent trait of his intellectual character was that moral courage which enables its possessor to follow his chosen purpose, regardless alike of the laugh of the low and the sneers of the lofty. It was founded on a strong sense of right and an intense love of truth, with no single feature of that dogged obstinacy, so much mistaken for it, which springs solely from pride and self-will.

As an observer, he was remarkably accurate and comprehensive. In this respect, his mind was characterized by that kind of shrewdness which detects analogies and diversities too subtle to be discerned by coarser intellects, rather than that philosophical insight which discovers the whole significance of a fact, long before all its incidents are accurately known. To the physician, the former quality is indispensable for the highest degree of success. Without it, every case, as it comes, must appear to be insulated from all others, a study by itself, in fact, without relation or bond of affinity to any other. Without it, the common element, the essential condition, is overlooked amid a multiplicity of particulars, and the process of generalization, which marks the first step of the reasoning power, in all philosophical induction, is deprived of its surest guide. I cannot forbear, in illustration of these remarks, to call your attention to a point most happily made in his opinion in the celebrated Parish will case. The essential question in this case was, whether the apparent loss of all intellectual power which followed a stroke of paralysis, was indicative of complete dementia, or only an accidental consequence of the loss of speech coincident with it, and therefore merely apparent. In the course of his discussion, which will amply repay a careful perusal, he adverted to a particular symptom stated in evidence, which, though it was apparently trivial, and had escaped the notice of other experts, he pronounced emphatically to be pathognomonic of dementia; and I apprehend that no one, after considering the fact by the light of his own experience, would dissent from his conclusion.

And yet I would not have it understood that he was particularly deficient in that higher exercise of the intellect, by which it arrives at results by a kind of intuitive perception. It was not very apparent in his writings, for they were designed to effect their purpose by the irresistible logic of facts, rather than by any refinements of speculation; but his conversation furnished abundant proof that he possessed it in no small degree. An apparently casual remark thrown out in the course of discussion, often showed that his mind had ranged far beyond the immediate bearings of the

question, and discerned conclusions which only time
and fresh inquiry could reveal to others.

Earnest as he was in his own beliefs, he allowed the
largest liberty of belief to others, and it was not his
way to attribute a difference of opinion to stupidity or
dishonesty. He had none of the proselyting spirit, and
thought no less kindly nor respectfully of any one
merely for differing from him in politics, religion, or
science. He always manifested a delicate reserve
towards the views of others when unlike his own, and
in company was studiously cautious how he advanced
opinions which he knew to be distasteful to the hum-
blest individual. Not even the opportunities of inti-
mate friendship were ever used by him to urge his
convictions upon others, however dear they might be
to him. On suitable occasions however, when to
refrain would have been culpable remissness, no one
was more outspoken than he, and when the cause of
humanity required it, he could utter the sternest of
rebukes.

His talents were somewhat versatile, and under a
special training, he would undoubtedly have excelled
in many pursuits quite foreign to that which engrossed
the best years of his life. One of his college exercises
was written in verse; but I am inclined to think that
in after life he never courted the muse. He was no
mean draughtsman, though he seldom used the talent
for any artistic purpose, except, after the manner of
young men in college, to adorn the walls of stair-cases

and lecture-rooms, with the faces of the professors, not photographically accurate, but wonderfully like. In after years he would often while away the tedious pauses in the course of a trial, by sketching in this way some striking specimen of the face divine in the collection around him. He had given much attention to the principles and practice of architecture, and once was employed by his fellow-townsmen to prepare the plans of a church they were about to build. It stands not far from the place of his professional labors, and, though not strictly in accordance with the most fashionable taste, is, nevertheless, a worthy specimen of the art. He had a decided turn for mechanics, and possessed a natural dexterity which often served him a very useful purpose. It is related of him that when engaged in miscellaneous practice in New Hampshire, he was unexpectedly required, when away from home, to amputate a limb. He had no instruments with him, and the circumstances admitted of no delay, but out of the domestic utensils of his patient's humble abode, he soon extemporized the instruments he needed. A razor served for a knife, an old tenon saw was newly filed for sawing through the bone, and a darning needle was deprived of its temper and then twisted into the form of a tenaculum. Many years later, the patient was seen topping out a tall chimney, in his vocation of bricklayer, supported on a wooden leg which the doctor had carved out for him with his own hands. While residing in New York, before removing to Derry, his mind was much occupied with mechanical inventions, among which was a machine for spinning flax. This was so far perfected that one of his friends, who had some part in suggesting or constructing it, took it to England in order to dispose of it, but was diverted from the purpose by some more promising enterprise, and it came to nothing.

The moral endowments of Dr. Bell were no less concerned than his intellectual, in making him a useful man and an honor to his race. A love of the right, the true, and the good, irrespective of all conventional distinctions, was the vital principle of his moral life. A mean, sordid, or dishonorable act was as remote from his nature as the poles are asunder, and his conduct was habitually governed by motives of the most elevated character. If his extensive knowledge of men prevented any childlike faith in human rectitude, it did not limit his indulgence to their faults, nor lead to a cynical distrust of all apparent virtue. His professional duties brought him into contact with all sorts and conditions of men, thus making him familiar with the darker aspects of our nature, but such experience did not harden his heart. It rather led him to look on vice and crime as a subject of curious and most important study with reference to their proper treatment by governments and individuals, which, he was disposed to think, should embrace but little of the vindictive element. To this view he was led, not more by his views respecting the relations of vice to organic imperfection, than by the all-pervading kindness of his nature. In fact, he belonged to the school of Burke when he took into his house the poor outcast who accosted him in the street, instead of handing her over to the police. To the sons and daughters of affliction and misfortune his hand and heart were ever open, and though not very demonstrative in his feelings, they were none the less warm and active. His kindness and exemption from sordid motives were strikingly manifested in his professional engagements, for he seemed to be equally ready to devote his time and talents to the service of those who could give him little or no compensation, as of those who could reward him according to their value. He was averse to detraction and ill-natured remark, and was more fond of dwelling upon the merits of others than upon their faults and short-comings. For his friends, no efforts, no sacrifices seemed too great; and even when they travelled the same path and might be supposed to be in his way, I believe no twinge of jealousy ever disturbed the genial current of his affections. He had not a particle of that spirit which seeks to keep down others, and promote one's own advancement by retarding theirs.

His evenness of temper under the strongest provocations was a remarkable trait in his character. Personal wrong and injustice might raise in him a feeling of indignation, as readily as in other men, but they failed to excite any violence of passion, or vindictive impulse. This trait was accompanied by another of a kindred nature — patience under trials both large and small — and from their mingled operation were evolved those graces of character which belong only to the chosen few. Many a man who encounters the great troubles of life without a murmur, like the inevitable processes of nature, is disturbed and irritated by the little annoyances, which, more or less, beset the path of every child of Adam. Our friend belonged to that small class who are as little moved by the one as the other. Whether the trial came in the shape of detention on the road while on his way to meet an important appointment, or of a gross perversion of his evidence by some unscrupulous lawyer; of a swindling attempt on his purse, or of a paragraph of misrepresentation and abuse in the newspaper; he preserved the serenity of his mind. Disease, and especially that form of it which afflicted him for many years, never produced that irritability which so often accompanies it; and at those moments when a man might well be pardoned for thinking only of himself, he was particularly thoughtful of others.

At all periods of his life, he evinced the same power of accommodating himself to circumstances, which was so remarkably displayed in the last phase of his career. While to a casual observer he may have appeared to be strongly attached to a customary routine, no man, in fact, ever departed from it more readily, even to the point of a considerable sacrifice, when moved by an adequate motive. The little accidents of life on which the comfort of most men so largely depends, he could readily disregard when the exigency required it.

To a stranger his manner often seemed cold, if not forbidding; wanting, at least, in what the French call *empressement.* It certainly was not marked by enthusiasm or superfluous warmth, but all who had the pleasure of his acquaintance became profoundly impressed, sooner or later, with the conviction of his thorough sincerity and cordiality. Frequently indeed, even to a stranger, there was an irresistible charm in his manner that rendered an interview with him a matter of pleasing recollection. Though utterly exempt from all manner of parade, affectation, and self-conceit, yet, in whatever company he might be found, there was always a certain dignity in his manners, which, without repelling the cordial advances of any, commanded the respect and regard of all. In his intercourse with others, he invariably manifested the utmost respect for their rights, was always scrupulously careful of their feelings, and never, to my knowledge, uttered an irritating remark, although a strong sense of the humorous was a prominent trait of his intellectual character. With all his ability he manifested the gentleness of a child, and, contrary to the usual course, I apprehend, the older he grew, the more gentle, the more patient, the more forbearing, the more tender, he became. Never were these traits so beautifully manifested, as they were in the closing scenes of his life. At the very moment when he was anticipating, as he had not for many

years, a future of improved health and a higher sphere
of usefulness, his hopes were suddenly dashed to the
ground, and he saw, as clearly as others, that the end
was at hand. On a hard pallet, under a canvas roof,
laid, for six days in the month of February, this delicate
invalid, who had repeatedly experienced the number-
less comforts of the sick-room, always within reach of
ample means. Yet no word of murmuring, or regret, or
repining, escaped his lips. He seldom spoke, except to
express his thanks to those who attended upon him ;
and thus he passed away, gently and serenely as he
had lived.

Such were the life and character of our departed
friend, feebly and imperfectly portrayed, I fear, but
certainly without exaggeration. It needs an abler
pen than mine to do full justice to his merits — to present him exactly as he was, an harmonious and happy
embodiment of those traits which exalt and adorn our
nature, ennobled and hallowed by faith in God and
the hope of immortality.